For Jabari, Mariama, Booker, Nia,
and all my young cousins
—*V. W.*

For my special gift, Whitney
—*S. W.*

*T*his is *not* going to be a good day," June said to herself as she sat on the back porch peeling red apples. The day was June 19. The year was 1943. A cool breeze blew, and the Texas sun toasted the top of June's head. She could hear the squeak of Aunt Marshall's rocking chair and the soft song her mother hummed as she rolled out the crust for an apple pie.

June glanced down the road that stretched in front of her like a long, dusty ribbon. Her father was coming home today, just in time for Juneteenth. He'd left two weeks ago for New York City. Before he'd left, June had traced his route with her finger on his old, wrinkled map.

Freedom's Gifts

A Juneteenth Story

By Valerie Wesley ~ Illustrated by Sharon Wilson

Simon & Schuster Books for Young Readers

SIMON & SCHUSTER BOOKS FOR YOUNG READERS
An imprint of Simon & Schuster Children's Publishing Division
1230 Avenue of the Americas, New York, New York 10020
Text copyright © 1997 by Valerie Wesley
Illustrations copyright © 1997 by Sharon Wilson
All rights reserved including the right of reproduction
in whole or in part in any form.
SIMON & SCHUSTER BOOKS FOR YOUNG READERS
is a trademark of Simon & Schuster.
Book design by Paul Zakris
The text of this book is set in 14-point Adobe Garamond
The illustrations are rendered in pastels
Printed and bound in Hong Kong
by South China Printing Company (1988) Ltd.
First Edition
10 9 8 7 6 5 4 3 2 1

Library of Congress Cataloging-in-Publication Data

Wesley, Valerie.
Freedom's gifts / by Valerie Wesley ;
illustrated by Sharon Wilson. — 1st ed.
p.   cm.
Summary: When a girl from New York visits her cousin in Texas,
she learns the origin of Juneteenth, a holiday marking the day
Texan slaves realized they were free.
ISBN 0-689-80269-2
[1. Afro-Americans—Social life and customs—Fiction. 2. Slavery—Texas—
Fiction. 3. Texas—Social life and customs—Fiction. 4. Juneteenth—Fiction.
5. Cousins—Fiction.] I. Wilson, Sharon (Sharon R.), 1954–   ill. II. Title.
PZ7.W515Fr   1997   [Fic]—dc20   96-24614   CIP   AC

Each year June's father made the trip to New York City to pick up her cousin Lillie. Lillie usually came to visit in August, but this time she was coming earlier and staying longer. When June thought about Lillie, her mouth puckered up tight as if she'd sucked on a lemon.

"Are you finished with those apples yet? I want to get the pie in the oven," June's mother called from the kitchen.

"Almost," June answered.

"When I was your age," Aunt Marshall said to June, "I would have peeled two dozen apples by now. And sugared 'em, baked 'em, served 'em, and cleaned up after 'em, too." Aunt Marshall stopped rocking and peered over her glasses at June. "But now I'm my age, and I don't have to do nothing but rock."

Aunt Marshall was June's great-great-aunt. Her voice was scratchy and low and sounded like her creaky rocking chair. Most days Aunt Marshall just rocked in her chair, "rememberin'." But sometimes Aunt Marshall talked about what her life had been like when she was June's age. She loved to talk about her sister, Sophie, and all the other kinfolk who had died long before June was born. June enjoyed listening to Aunt Marshall's tales.

Aunt Marshall was very old. Some people said she was the oldest woman in Texas. She was born when African Americans were enslaved and records of their births and deaths were not kept. She was about the same age as June when the first Juneteenth was celebrated—June 19, 1865, the day when black people who lived in Texas were finally set free.

"Shhh, hush!" Aunt Marshall said suddenly, and tilted her head as if listening to something far away. June listened, too. She heard the rumbling sound of her father's red truck as it turned the last bend in the road.

"He's home, Mama, he's home!" June jumped up from her apple peeling and ran down the steps toward the truck, which stopped right in front of her in a swirl of dust. Her father laughed as he jumped out of the cab and gave her a kiss.

"How's my Junebug doing?" he asked. "Junebug, say hello to your cousin Lillie. She's had a hard trip coming down here, a long, *long* trip," her father said in one breath. "But we made it back. Just in time for the Juneteenth picnic. You ready for the Juneteenth picnic, Junebug?" he asked with a smile. June smiled back and nodded that she was.

"My, how you've grown, Lillie," June's mother said when she came from the kitchen and gave Lillie a hug. Lillie *did* look grown, June thought to herself. Just like a teenager. "June, why don't you take Lillie into the house so she can put away her bags and freshen up before the picnic," June's mother said as she gave Lillie a gentle shove toward June. June made herself smile. Lillie wouldn't smile back.

"I don't like Texas," Lillie said, and poked out her mouth.

"You girls hurry up now, so we can eat some of that good food your mama's been cooking for Juneteenth," June's father said. June took one of Lillie's bags and Lillie took the other. Then the girls headed into the house.

Aunt Marshall and June shared a room. Their beds stood together like two good friends.

"That's Aunt Marshall's bed," June warned Lillie as she plopped down on her aunt's bed. "You better get off. You're going to sleep in my bed with me. Aunt Marshall doesn't like anybody sitting on her bed."

"You scared of her?" Lillie asked. "I'm not scared of anybody." But she jumped off Aunt Marshall's bed and onto June's, which began to wobble.

"I'm hungry," Lillie said as she slid to the floor. "Is it time to eat yet?"

"Pretty soon. We'll eat at the Juneteenth picnic," June answered.

"Juneteenth? What's that?"

"It's . . ." June paused. She never had to explain Juneteenth before. Everybody in Texas already knew what it was.

"Juneteenth is freedom day," she finally said, recalling what Aunt Marshall and her parents had told her. "It's the day the slaves in Texas were told they were free." She was glad she remembered. "Christmas is my favorite holiday, but I like Juneteenth better than Thanksgiving because there's food *and* a parade. And Juneteenth is better than Easter because my name is part of it. *June*teenth. That makes it special."

"The slaves must have been dumb not to know they were free," said Lillie.

June tossed her cousin a sideways glance. "Aunt Marshall's not dumb, and she didn't know she was free. They didn't know they were free because the masters kept it a secret. They wanted them to stay slaves so that they could make them work for free."

"So Juneteenth is a *slave* holiday," Lillie said firmly with a sniff. "Up North we celebrate the Fourth of July. That's why my daddy went North. So our family can be like everybody else. Not old-timey, like down here."

June didn't say anything, but her face felt hot.

Soon it was time to load the truck for the Juneteenth picnic. The girls took turns carrying out the blankets and baskets loaded with food. Aunt Marshall sat next to June's parents in the cab. June and Lillie spread a blanket out in the back of the truck and sat down on it.

June loved to ride in the back of the truck. She loved to feel the wind in her face and watch the clouds float by. When the day finally grew cool and the sky so dark you couldn't see, June loved to count the stars—one, two, three—and wish on them the way Aunt Marshall told her to. But there were no stars in the light of the day. If there had been, June knew what she would wish— that Lillie would go home.

"Why can't I ride with the grown-ups?" Lillie asked.

"I don't want to sit on this blanket, it smells," she complained.

"The wind is making my eyes hurt," she whined.

Lillie had just gotten to Texas and June was tired of her already.

As the truck pulled into the park, Lillie pointed to a large sign tacked near a water fountain as she spelled out the words.

"W-H-I-T-E-S O-N-L-Y. That sign spells 'whites only'!" Lillie said.

The sign was just like the ones that hung in the department stores and many other places. Those signs pointed to where June and her family could never go. June didn't think much about the signs. It was just the way things were.

"Does the sign mean we can't drink the water that comes out of that water fountain?" Lillie asked. She sounded confused. "Does that mean we can't drink the same water as white children?

"I'm glad I'm not from down here. Up North, we can do what we want to do and go where we want to go. We can drink anywhere we want to drink. Living here is like being a slave who can't go where she wants to go and do what she wants to do. Living in the South makes you like a slave, June. A dumb old slave. Just like Juneteenth—a dumb old slave holiday!"

June shifted her eyes away from her cousin's. She'd never thought much about the signs, but now they made her feel ashamed, even though they weren't her fault.

The red truck pulled into the spot in the park where everybody had gathered for the Juneteenth picnic, but June couldn't forget Lillie's hurtful words. They stung her like a slap. June thought about what Lillie had said when they climbed out of the truck and ran to the bandstand to see what they could see. She thought about them as the marching band from Carver High stood straight and tall and strutted their stuff when they marched. She could still hear them as the cymbals and drums clashed like thunder in the bright afternoon and when the ladies dressed in white from the Tubman Ladies Aid Society strolled through the crowd, offering kind words and comfort to those who needed them.

June remembered what Lillie had said as
her parents and the others spread food on
the long tables so everybody could help
themselves. June could smell jambalaya, corn
bread, sausage, and the sweet pies made with
the apples she'd peeled. But Lillie's words had
left a sour taste in June's mouth. The taste
was still there when June dropped down on
the blanket next to Aunt Marshall.

"Where's that sassy little something that
reminds me of my sister, Sophie?" Aunt
Marshall asked. "Go get that little girl Lillie."

Lillie was sitting on a blanket far away
from everybody else. There was a plate of
food beside her, but Lillie hadn't eaten. June
wondered if Lillie hadn't eaten because she
was homesick.

"Aunt Marshall wants to see you," she said
to Lillie.

"Why?" Lillie asked with a pout.

"I don't know, but you better come.
Everybody does what Aunt Marshall says,
even Mama," June warned. Lillie poked her
mouth out further but followed June back to
where Aunt Marshall sat.

"Sit down a spell and keep me company," Aunt Marshall said to Lillie with a wink. June folded her arms tight. She thought that Aunt Marshall only winked at her.

"You're just like my big sister, Sophie, when we was young like you-all are now," Aunt Marshall said to Lillie. "You got the same pretty eyes and the same frisky spirit. She was smart as an old goose, though, and couldn't nobody tell what was going to come out that girl's mouth."

Lillie smiled a tiny smile.

"You're just like Sophie come back," Aunt Marshall said.

"What happened to her, to Sophie?" Lillie asked.

"Gone—just like the rest of them," Aunt Marshall said quietly. "The two of you sitting together reminds me of me and Sophie, that day she found me and all we had was each other."

"Were you lost?" Lillie asked. The pout was gone, and June could see concern in Lillie's eyes.

"Before that first Juneteenth, before freedom came," Aunt Marshall answered.

"Tell us what it was like before freedom came?" June asked. June had heard the story before, but she loved to listen to Aunt Marshall tell it.

Aunt Marshall didn't say anything for a while. "Juneteenth always sets me to rememberin'. Those times were ugly, filled with so much evil and meanness, I don't even want to think about them on a day as good as this one. We were born grown back then—at least we felt it," she said softly, and her eyes got the faraway look, the "rememberin'" look that usually told June she didn't want to be bothered. But Aunt Marshall was talking now. June stole a glance at Lillie, who listened, too.

A butterfly swooped down from a stalk of weed to a flower and then finally to a twig that lay in the grass. "She is freer than we were then." Aunt Marshall nodded toward the butterfly. "A bluebird. An ant that could crawl where it wanted. You had nothing but your mama's arms or your sister's to warm up to at night, and them that owned you could take your family away anytime they wanted. Like they did my big sister. My Sophie."

A look of sadness crossed Aunt Marshall's face, and June could see the sparkle of a tear in her eye. June knew that she was thinking of things it hurt her to remember. She was sorry that she had asked Aunt Marshall about those old times.

"But they couldn't take your thoughts, the way your mama sung softly to you, or the way your sister's arms felt against yours. I kept them close and tight within me."

"And then freedom came?" Lillie asked.

"Finally. Two and a half years after everybody else was free," June answered, remembering what she'd already learned about that first Juneteenth.

"What happened that day, Aunt Marshall?" Lillie asked, and June realized that Lillie had never heard Aunt Marshall's story.

"I was in the barn that day," Aunt Marshall said, "gathering some eggs. I heard all this laughing and shouting and carrying on, folks screaming out like they'd lost their minds. I was scared to come out, they was making so much commotion. But I was just a little 'un, I didn't know what freedom meant. Everybody was looking for kin who'd been lost or sold or snatched. Mamas for their babies, husbands for their wives. Then Sophie found me, and I knew it must be true. That freedom *had* come. 'We're free, Marshall! Free. Free. Free!' Sophie told me. And then she laughed. I'll remember that laugh, so sweet and deep, until the day I die."

"Are we free now?" June asked.

"Freer than we was," Aunt Marshall said.

"But that's not free. Or we could drink water wherever we want, not just where the sign tells us to," Lillie said angrily.

"We're free as I'll be in this lifetime. Free as I'll be before I die. But not as free as you'll be someday," Aunt Marshall said quietly, and nodded toward Lillie. "You all have freedom's gifts, and can't nobody take them away."

Lillie and June sat beside Aunt Marshall for a few more minutes. June felt sad when she thought about Aunt Marshall's tale, but she felt special, too. She glanced at Lillie. She couldn't tell if Lillie felt like she did or what was going to come out of her mouth. Just like Aunt Marshall and Sophie.

"Want to play?" Lillie asked after a minute. June nodded. The girls sat on the hot ground and played while the ladies from the Tubman Ladies Aid Society gathered up their baskets, until the band had put away their instruments, and after the Juneteenth sun had set pink and yellow in the Texas sky. Then the two girls helped load the truck.

It was dark and quiet in the back of the truck as June and Lillie lay side by side on the ride home. June thought about the butterfly that had been freer than Aunt Marshall and the water fountain that only white people could drink from. And then she thought about freedom's gifts, and how they would belong to her and Lillie like they never had belonged to Aunt Marshall and Sophie. That made her feel proud and just a little sad, too.

"You asleep?" Lillie asked.

"Are you?" June asked back.

"Would I ask you if I were?" Lillie said like she was mad, but then she laughed. June laughed, too, and wondered if Lillie's laugh was like Sophie's used to be—the sweet, deep one that Aunt Marshall would never forget.

"I'm going to ask my daddy if I can come down here in June from now on. We don't have anything like Juneteenth up North," Lillie said after a minute.

June didn't say anything; she just smiled to herself. Juneteenth, she decided, had been as good as a June day could be.

Author's Note

Juneteenth commemorates the emancipation of African Americans in Texas. The Emancipation Proclamation, issued by Abraham Lincoln on January 1, 1863, did not bring freedom to all slaves. African Americans remained enslaved in Texas. Some people believe it was because the masters didn't want to free their slaves. Others say it was because the news was slow to reach Texas. On June 19, 1865, General Gordon Granger landed on Galveston Island and proclaimed the sovereignty of the United States over Texas and the freedom of all who had been enslaved—two and a half years after slavery had ended in other parts of the South. From that day on, the nineteenth of June was celebrated by black Texans with picnics and parades. Juneteenth was made a Texas state holiday in 1979. Today Juneteenth is celebrated by African Americans in many parts of the United States.

—V. W.